# Farmer George
## and the Hungry Guests

Other titles featuring
Farmer George are:

*Farmer George
and the Fieldmice*

*Farmer George
and the Lost Chick*

*Farmer George
and the Hedgehogs*

*Farmer George
and the Snowstorm*

*Farmer George
and the New Piglet*

# Farmer George
## and the Hungry Guests

# Nick Ward

PAVILION

First published in Great Britain in 1999 by
PAVILION BOOKS LIMITED
London House, Great Eastern Wharf
Parkgate Road, London SW11 4NQ

This edition published 2001

Designed by Ness Wood at Zoom Design

A CIP catalogue record for this book is available
from the British Library.

ISBN 1 86205 531 9

Set in Bell MT
Printed and bound in Singapore by Kyodo
Colour origination in Hong Kong by AGP Repro (HK) Ltd.

2 4 6 8 10 9 7 5 3 1

This book can be ordered direct from the publisher. Please contact
the Marketing Department. But try your bookshop first.

"I'm hungry," said Farmer George. It was early in the morning and he had just finished milking Hermione. He wanted his breakfast. "I think I'll have a nice boiled egg and soldiers," he smiled. "Come on Tam."

But when Farmer George searched the hen house, he couldn't find a single egg! "That's strange," he thought. "Never mind, I'll have a duck's egg instead."

But the ducks had no eggs either! They were very puzzled. "Quack," they cried. "I'm sure we laid some eggs!" "Oh dear," said Farmer George. "I'll have to have some cereal instead." And he marched back to the cow shed to get some milk.

"I don't know what's going on, Hermione," said Farmer George to his favourite cow. "There are no eggs for my breakfast. Whatever next?" Farmer George lifted the lid of the milk churn and dipped the ladle inside. "Well I never," he cried. The milk churn was empty!

"I think we have an uninvited guest Tam," said Farmer George. "Let's go and investigate."

"Have you seen anything strange?" he asked all the animals.

"NO!" they quacked, bleated, grunted
and mooed.

"But my sugar lumps have vanished
as well," neighed Sidney.

Tam and Farmer George went to look for clues. "Look Tam," said Farmer George, pointing to a loose plank in the grain store. "Let's look inside."

Inside the store they discovered a bag of oats was missing. Farmer George took out his scissors. "This should do the trick," he smiled, and snipped off a corner of the remaining bag. "Now Tam, this is my plan…"

Early next morning, Tam was hiding
in the hen house. He saw a small
brown paw reach through a hole in the

wall and take three brown eggs! Tam
crept off to find Farmer George...

...who was hiding behind the grain store. "Ssh Tam," whispered Farmer George.

Soon they heard the sound of the loose plank being lifted, and then the pattering of hurrying paws.

Farmer George switched
on his torch and saw a
thin trail of oats.

"Just as I thought. Come on Tam," he
said, following the trail across the yard,

and over the field to a spinney.

The trail disappeared into a hole
in the side of a large mound of grass.
"Ssh," whispered Farmer George.

Just as the sun was rising, they peered through a crack in the side of the mound, and saw a family of hungry foxes!

"So they're our hungry guests," grinned Farmer George. "And enjoying a breakfast of porridge and eggs!"

"In my bowl!" whimpered Tam.

Farmer George and Tam walked home in the early morning sunshine. "We must do something for those little foxes," said Farmer George.

And he did! Every evening he left a basket of goodies by the back door for his guests...

...making sure he'd saved enough eggs for his own breakfast!

# Which trail of oats will lead Farmer George to the foxes' home?